Charles Wood Chapman

The Vision of Socrates

And other Poems

Charles Wood Chapman

The Vision of Socrates
And other Poems

ISBN/EAN: 9783337397708

Printed in Europe, USA, Canada, Australia, Japan

Cover: Foto ©Andreas Hilbeck / pixelio.de

More available books at **www.hansebooks.com**

THE

VISION OF SOCRATES,

AND OTHER

POEMS.

BY

CHARLES WOOD CHAPMAN.

𝔏𝔬𝔫𝔡𝔬𝔫 :

PROVOST & CO. (successors to A. W. BENNETT,

5, BISHOPSGATE WITHOUT.

MDCCCLXIX.

CONTENTS.

THE VISION OF SOCRATES.

In proud Athenia, where of old began
    The arts and sciences to rear their throne,
He who the grandest victories had won,
    Was, for his greatness, doomed by death t'atone.

Within a dungeon's solitary gloom,
    Rapt in profound philosophy he stood ;
Beheld the fields where heightened glories bloom,
    And passed by faith the intervening flood.

B

'Twas naught to him that the remorseless crowd
    Besought his death for too sublime a life;
When nature's noblest sons before him bowed,
    And spirits hailed him from so mean a strife.

E'en now descending from the realms of light
    A heavenly messenger propitious came,
And as she spoke the prisoner's eye waxed bright,
    And in his soul glowed an immortal flame.

A mortal's wanderings through the tracts of air,—
    The secrets of the future state she sung;
And when she showed the crowns awarded there,
    The dim old chamber to the echo rung.

THE SPIRIT'S SONG.

ASPIRING mortal! as the moments fly,—
The heralds of thy glorious destiny,—
In tranquil rest, upon thy couch repose,
For here shall end the sum of all thy woes.
But what of noble patience thou hast won,
The lofty march which thou hast here begun,
Shall win for thee in the celestial race
Unfading laurels and a victor's place:
A vision of that future I reveal,
And hence prepare thee for thy last ordeal.

Enveloped in this planetary sphere—
Which Sol controls and guides the rolling year—
Vast bodies in harmonious concert turn,
And mimic suns their winding course adorn;
Some banished from the sacred source of light,
Are doomed to bitter frosts and wasting blight;
While others, nurtured by a warmer air,
A bounteous feast for man and beast prepare.
But one there is, more favoured than the rest,
The choicest riches yields—the portion of the blest—
Where joyful souls through winning landscapes roam:
Such is the clime I sing, and such thy future home.
Within that world a lovely land there lies,
Viewed by angelic, hid from human eyes;
A fairy island floating in the main,
Long for its beauty known without a name:
Here spirits of a higher order meet
From tracts beyond our view, from heaven's
     celestial seat;
In sacred groves and vallies they converse,

And raise their voices in harmonious verse;
To them 'tis given to pierce earth's dark abodes,
And, swift as airy thought, the palaces of gods.

    Now evening spreads her pinions o'er the isle
Of high enchantment, and the sun's last smile
Lives in the firmament, the wild winds sleep
Within their caves, and o'er the placid deep
Walks forth the queen of beauty, robed in white,
Wooed by the silent eloquence of night;
When on the borders of the tranquil flood,
Locked arm in arm, two bright celestials stood.

    The high behest, Adoria, which I bring,
The elder cried, from heaven's omniscient King,
Permits our souls sweet friendship to renew,
And sister in itself, is doubly dear to you.

    A stranger, on the Adriatic shore,
His lowly lot and being doth deplore,
Longs to precipitate the wheels of fate,
And pierce the mist profound that hides his future
      state;

The dwarft ambition of his grovelling race,

In his aspiring mind commands no place;

But ocean, mountain, and the glittering star,

Have voices know to him—to him familiar are;

Then smiling hope the shrouded landscape clears,

A purer clime, another race appears;

Bright fields of fancy open to his view,

For ever beautiful and ever new;

The soul emboldened lifts her fervent eye,

And hails her home and claims her destiny;

Though clogged by matter, groping in the dark,

Oh! more than mortal is that vital spark:

To you the choice prerogative I bear,

To guide him through the subtle tracts of air;

The mystic wonders of your state to tell,

And show the fields where happy spirits dwell.

No more she said, but passing like a ray

The fairy bounds, in distance died away.

    Meanwhile, Adolphus, fixed in earnest thought,

The whispering woods and wavy ocean sought:

Oh! when will this protracted struggle cease,

At length he cried, and I repose in peace ;

The lingering pangs and doubts of life be o'er,

And I disbark upon a calmer shore ;

This world's vain pageants fade before my eyes,

Or heard as murmurs of departing tides ?

For oft entranced in lofty faith, I deem

Its joys a bubble and its hopes a dream.

Ye spirits who pervade the silent night,

Ye souls who dwell in yonder worlds of light,

Am I too mean, too weak a wretch, to claim

Your breath to kindle an immortal flame?

Perchance, amid your shining throngs, are seen

Transported souls who on this world have
       been ;

Borne toil and anguish, and the ills of life,

Espoused the good, and conquered in the strife ;

Who, bending from their lofty thrones, descry

A mortal's woes with sympathetic eye,

And moved by love, which they alone can know,

Forsake the skies for thorny paths below,

To guide the erring step, bid sorrow cease to flow.

　　As thus he speaks, a flood of golden light

Breaks o'er the landscape and dispels the night;

Enchanting music sweeps the woods among,

And voices from on high the tuneful notes prolong;

The distance lessening, nearer and more near

The sweet Adoria and her maids appear,

Form a bright circle on the rosy main,

Herself the foremost of the gifted train.

In dread suspense, Adolphus trembling stood,

And watched their progress o'er the crystal flood;

Their liquid eyes and ivory bosoms bare,

The music of their step and more than mortal air,

The hovering glories that their presence grace,

Bespeaks them nymphs of an exalted race.

To fall and worship was at first his bent;

But when her charm the fond ethereal lent,

Time, matter, sense, the spreading sea and land

Swept from his view as 'neath a fairy's wand;

The boundless soul, her boundless empire sought,
Rapt in the vast eternity of thought.

Then thus the heavenly messenger : Arise,
Weak child of earth, and claim thy native skies,
Nor longer hope unaided to explore
The maze of truth on this benighted shore,
The blissful climes where favoured souls reside
Lie open now, myself will be your guide;
To pass the immeasurable space between
That world and this, is but a fleeting dream;
Rise, cast thy bonds of lethargy away,
And, disembodied, seek the realms of day.

She said, and touched him with her gentle hand,
And led him to the margin of the strand;
They leave the shore and forest gloom behind,
The restless deep and the more troubled wind;
An eagle glancing through the liquid air,
Nor lightning, with their swiftness may compare.
At length, recovering from his first surprise,
Adolphus gazed about with anxious eyes:

Beheld the earth by subtle ether bound,

And flaming worlds above, and empty space around.

Then, to his bright compeer: Say, gracious power,

Who dawn'st on me in a propitious hour,

What led so high intelligence to take

This dreary flight, and purer climes forsake ?

Can wretched man exulting spirits move,

And touch the chord of universal love ?

Or, in obedience to supreme command,

Leave you the blissful seats, and tread earth's

   barren sand ?

  She answered thus : The irrevocable will

Of our Creator we with haste fulfil ;

Nor less the secret pleasure that we feel,

His fixed behest and purpose to reveal ;

Nor wonder that we willingly forego

The blooming fields above for desert wastes below.

Implanted in the loftiest seraph's soul,

Unconquerable love asserts control ;

In the full pulse of varied nature glows,

And from the fount of vital goodness flows.

Subduing pity and persuasive love

Water, with pleading tears, the shining courts above;

Before the throne of awful justice stand,

And stay His lightning darts, the thunders of His
    hand ;

The invincible ambassadors are they

Of Him who holds all worlds beneath His sway :

Hence, spirit guests, through the revolving hours,

Pass and repass, from heaven's enchanting bowers;

Borne on the spreading wings of light sublime

They pierce the aërial void, nor heed the flight of
    time :

In all the worlds to training mortals given,

In all the spheres that through this vast are driven,

Meet the symphonious throngs—the denizens of
    heaven ;

Nor deem the separation is so great

Between our own and your more transient state :

To those who battle with the growing wrong,

Triumphant strains and victor's crowns belong.

We mark the progress of the generous flame,

For such has been our lot, our victory the same;

To-day they mingle with the moving crowd,

Their energies benumbed, by lifeless matter bowed;

To-morrow they ennobling airs respire,

Assume the vacant seat, and quaff celestial fire:

Guided by starry faith, O who would grieve

Yon waning world and wintry clime to leave,

Such bliss to share, such trophies to receive?

　　She paused, and on Adolphus fixed her look,

And all the Godhead in his nature woke:

O source benign, he cried, thy accents, clear

As springs in deserts, greet my lingering ear:

Oft in the solitary shades of night,

With the pale moon to guide my steps aright,

A voice hath fired me with these truths sublime,

And stole a march on scarce-recording time;

Yet so remote those passing whispers were,

While so complete thy revelations are,

Still heightened by this boundless theatre,

That did not matchless goodness at this hour

Uphold me, I should sink beneath their power:

But now, confiding in mid space, I stand,

With countless worlds revolving on each hand,

Nor more of terror doth my soul partake

Than infant wonder on a sunny lake.

As thus communing they the moments spend,

They draw unconscious toward their journey's end;

The massive deep and mountain tops appear,

More dense becomes the partial atmosphere;

Then crowning woods and pearly brooks are seen,

And plains and vallies clothed in living green;

The orient morn salutes the crowding waves,

And night, with stealthy step, flies to her silent

      caves:

Full on a promontory's lofty height

The sister spirits and their guest alight.

The favoured clime, where blissful anthems ring,

And beauty walks her annual round, I sing;

Where souls, unmindful of their former woes,
New life embrace, and breathe a long repose ;
There, day and night divide the happy reign,
And silver-footed eve glides o'er the grassy plain.
The maiden Spring, with downcast eyes and slow,
Breathes her soft influence on the flowers that grow ;
The music of her step at times is heard,
And rustling robes by gentle zephyrs stirred ;
But queen-like Summer, with a numerous train,
Drives four white coursers o'er the burnished plain,
Her golden chariot is beheld from far,
And eyes more brilliant than the morning star ;
Then Autumn, in imperial purple dressed,
With fruits and viands to her bosom pressed,
Moves o'er the scene the universal friend,
And eager eyes her tardy steps attend :
But howling Winter, with his snowy locks,
Shorn forests, wasted fields, and bleating flocks,
Ne'er shows his blasted form or drifting sleet,
Nor felt his biting frost, nor heard his chattering teeth.

As thus the seasons in fair measure move,

The whole creation wears the purple light of
     love;

Clear flow the waters through the wealthy land;

The crested waves repose upon the golden sand;

There, mellow fruits to blushing branches cling;

Wakes perfume from the flowers, the birds in con-
     cert sing;

O'er man and beast, o'er ocean, earth, and sky,

Brood the soft wings of spell-bound harmony;

Oft in the deep recesses of the woods,

And on the confines of the murmuring floods,

Celestial beings linger in their flight,

Known by their graceful mien and crowns of
     circling light;

The mountains, vallies, and the hollow shore,

Rehearse the strains of their prophetic lore;

Charmed echo bears the lofty theme along,

The wondering nations crowd to catch the heavenly
     song:

A rapturous trance throughout the region runs,
And truths immortal from immortal tongues.

The pilgrim-guest a wide expanse beholds,
Graced with the tints the sylvan morn unfolds;
When lo ! the children of the clime are seen
To issue from their bowers of living green—
The stranger asked his guide from whence they
came,
What link they filled in the celestial chain?

These are the sons and daughters of your
earth,
Who held a servile place and claimed a lowly birth;
Bowed down by sorrow and laborious toil,
They turned the glebe and smoothed the knotty soil.
Through howling winds and heaven's inclemency,
Exposed and wet they plowed the stubborn lee—
Unmoved by warring tempests overhead,
Forced by their children's cry and craving want of
bread.
Their labour with the opening day begun,

And scarcely ended with the setting sun ;
And when the autumn opes the nursing year,
And wavy crops of golden corn appear,
They plied the sickle on the burning field,
And reaped for feudal lords the wealthy yield:
But mid their toils and sufferings they cried
To Him who for the raven doth provide,
Who holds the scales of empires in His hand,
And guides the rolling spheres, and rules the sub-
    ject land ;
Upon His gracious attributes reposed,
In peaceful death their weary eyelids closed :
Trusting a Father's love they journeyed on,
And hence the boon their patient faith hath won.

    But come with me, thy trembling mind enfold
In new born strength new wonders to behold ;
For not the shepherd by the murmuring stream,
Nor happy swains who of to-morrow dream,
Partake alone the bounties of the clime,
But those there are endowed with souls sublime.

Patriots and kings, and princes of your earth,

Re-animated, rise and own a second birth ;

The virtuous, good, and noble reunite,

And add fresh glories to the realms of light :

They draw the homage of the gazing throng,

As with majestic step they move along —

These are the powers who o'er the planet reign,

And all acknowledge their superior claim.

Now cast your eyes around this wide expanse,

And mark each object with attentive glance :

You see the domes and palaces, that crowd

Yon river's banks, with turrets high and proud ;

Some from the vales and sloping ground arise ;

Some on the hilly tops are lost in ambient skies ;

Some, shrouded by the foliage of the trees,

Are favoured with a cold refreshing breeze ;

While those which grace the lofty mountain's brow,

Command a prospect of the plains below —

The ocean's ample breast and morning's purple glow.

The sons of peace inhabit these abodes,

Who shun the pressing crowd and fortune's rugged
    roads;
No thoughts vindictive o'er their bosoms sweep,
No troubled dreams invade the calm of sleep;
The joys of home, their children's winning smile,
And charms of nature leisure hours beguile;
And when they gather round the social board,
And He the bounteous giver is adored,
The choicest dainties that the lands produce
Are gathered for their own peculiar use;
The sumptuous feast with rosy wine is crowned,
Ambrosial fruits and treasured gifts go round,
And sweet contentment in the dome is found.
Discord and hate, nor coldness, e'er pervade
Those charmed assemblies, nor deceits are laid,
But noble candour lights each lofty brow,
And the soul ratifies each whispered vow.

    The laws of teeming matter some explore,
And probe the source of philosophic lore:
The lightning's vivid flash, the martial tread

Of rattling thunder, with its bolts of dread;
The varied strata of our mother earth;
The countless progeny to which her womb gives
      birth;
The rise of rivers, ocean's ebb and flow,
Her wrinkled form above, her calm repose below;
The restless winds, the tempered atmosphere;
Spring, with her timid smile, and autumn's hearty
      cheer;
The innumerable stars, and sweeping train,
The order of their march, the magic chain
That binds the whole, their rapt attention claim.
But more, the texture of the hidden soul,—
Her distant origin, and future goal:
That vital principle which knows no bounds,
But worlds of fancy and of fact surrounds,
With daring energy drives thought on thought,
'Till the vast universe is 'neath its sceptre brought.
    Swayed by a noble aim on earth, they strove
To grasp at truth, and sophistry explode;

And though surrounded by a starless night,

They touched her mantle and proclaimed the right;

But now, with more redundant essence fired,

With spirits by their side, by spirit souls inspired,

They trace her passage through the liquid sky,

And pierce the web of shrouding mystery.

Could, from the cold dominion of the tomb,

The fond departed wake in youthful bloom,

Appear before her lover's ardent eyes,

And ope the sacred fount of golden memories,

Not with more rapture would his spirit burn

Than they, the student souls, the goal of truth
      discern.

    But see, the saffron morn hath opened wide

Heaven's orient gates, and pours a crimson tide;

And in the conscious majesty of might,

Rolls on his burnished car, the god of light.

The voices of a multitude I hear,

Like floods of circling music full and clear.

To view still more the beauty of this clime,

And learn the secrets of the state be thine.

As when, amid the islands of the west,

The crimson sun displays his brazen crest,

Unlocks the gates of fancy's fairy halls,

And to the brow of heaven the chief magician calls;

Swayed by the virtue of her potent wand,

Towers, battlements, and stately mansions stand;

Woods, plains, and mountains in succession rise;

The waters dance beneath the ambient skies,

'Till in habiliments of glory robed

All melt in one translucent sea of gold;

So broke the enchanting landscape on the sight,

Decked in celestial hues, and crowned with purple
    light.

Adolphus watched the ever-varying scene.

But thought it rather a delusive dream;

Such as enchantment loves to people sleep,

When home and sunny vales before the wanderer
    sweep,

Than gorgeous palaces and fixed abodes

Of favoured man and tranquil haunt of gods.

To him the heavenly monitor began:

These are the tenements of mortal man,

The groves and fountains where they oft repair,

And their's the rosy sky and balmy air ;

For He, who guided systems in their prime,

Breathes a soft halo o'er this fruitful clime.

Not so upon yon planetary earth;

There, blight, disease, and hurricanes have birth;

The germs of pestilence igniting roll,

And pointed lightnings flash from pole to pole;

The grateful promise of the year is borne

O'er flooded fields, or stricken by the storm,

And bursting on rich autumn's golden reign,

Mid winter whirls his tempests o'er the plain.

Such is the contrast in the rolling years,

But still more marked the races of the spheres,

For not an ill descends through nature's cause,

But is out-rivalled by immoral laws.

Do fierce contentions in the skies prevail—

Shrill whistling winds, and darts of poisoned hail,—
Man, by revenge and false ambition driven,
Outvies the blast and thunderbolts of heaven.

When throned presumptuous on his glittering
car,
He drives vindictive through the ranks of war,
What horrors track the ruthless homicide—
Death and affright, and desolation wide;
Pale nature shudders, for her teeming lands
And garnered grain is fired with flaming brands;
E'en helpless dames, and infants at the breast,
Have known the terrors of his fell behest;
Meantime the world, with an approving nod,
Looks on, and hails him as a victor-god.
But vain it were, and piteous to relate
The various evils nurtured by the state;
The cold intolerance and proud disdain
It shows the meaner subjects of its reign;
The scorned petition and the studied wrong;
Oppression to the weak, and flattery to the strong;

The guiltless victim to the law betrayed,

While guilt rides barefaced with his reeking blade;

The palsied miser, brooding on his store,

With meagre famine knocking at the door;

And, were this not enough, the vicious wear

The robes of virtue, and her sceptre bear.

Love, the sublimest attribute of God,

And patient dweller in yon mean abode,

Is made the harbinger of lawless lust,

And they who suffer worst most nobly trust.

Sad is the spectacle, that man who boasts

The highest order of created hosts,

Advances claims to an immortal race,

Should thus himself and fellow man debase.

    She said, and through the winning landscape

      moved

Where all creation seemed with life endued;

Earth, sky, and ocean, the united frame

Of mind and matter, own the genial flame;

The peerless Majesty of heaven adore,

Who is, and was, and reigns for evermore.

Sweet as the incense of an angel's breath,

When life hangs hovering on the brow of death,

The soft enchantment was; but when anew

The prospect stretched before the gazer's view;

When spread beneath the ken, a grassy plain

Rose from the close embraces of the main,

On which ten thousand matchless heroes stood,

Surrounded by a countless multitude,

Whose form, and stature, and commanding mein,

Marked them above the rest, and more than mortal

      men,—

Adolphus, turning to his guide, expressed

His new-born wonder, and these words addressed:

Say, Spirit, whence those lofty worthies came,

Who shine conspicuous on the velvet plain,

For well I deem that such celestial grace

Could never spring from earth's degenerate race.

     High o'er the crowd, upon your planet shone

These warrior chieftains, and as such were known;

The historian's pen, and poet's glowing song,

Their fame, their actions, and their worth prolong ;

Myriads unborn shall strive to emulate

The noble deeds of those who dared be great,

And gratitude, from age to age proclaim,

The conquerors over death, and call them each by

    name.

Not by vain glory and ambition led,

They rode amid the dying and the dead,

And sought by such empirical renown

To win an honoured place and lasting crown ;

Nor lightly drew they the avenging sword

For deeds of slaughter, which their souls abhorred,—

But when oppression to a mountain grew,

And pampered vice her baleful venom threw ;

When, chained within the pestilential cell,

The patriot saw the hopes of years dispel ;

When all the great and noble of the land

Were chased as deer, or bore an exile's brand ;

When servile flattery was the step to power,

And wrong triumphant stalked,—they chose the
    hour:
Throughout the regions blew a warning blast,
And on the crouching slave a royal mantle cast.
Then shook the people with a whirlwind's breath,
Then woke they from a torpor worse than death;
Then freedom in the van conspicuous shone,
And haughty tyrants trembled on their throne;
Those whose endeavours with success were crowned,
Triumphal arches and processions found,
Applauding senates all their actions name,
And death himself but consecrates their fame.

    But some there are, amid yon glittering throng,
Whose name ne'er echoed in the roll of song;
No silent mourners watched their honoured shade;
No marble columns rose above their grave;
And yet they were the noblest sons of earth,
Men whose capacious souls and peerless worth
Forbade them stoop with the degraded crowd,
And worship wrong grown arrogant and proud;

But in the midst of universal night,
When it were death to vindicate the right,
They chose the worthy part, as if to show
A God still ruling in the world below.

As thus, Adoria to her guest explained
The title there, still others pressed the plain;
Not in the panoply of arms they shone,
And yet they stood superior and alone;
Where'er they went their presence there was felt,
Crowds gathered and admired, and on each accent
       dwelt;
Such peerless beauty ne'er was seen till now,
Ne'er sat so rich a grace upon a mortal's brow;
Their matchless spirits threw a charm around,
Those who drew near by magic chords were bound;
The baser ailments of the being sunk,
And the whole soul celestial essence drunk.

These form a race, resumed the patient guide,
Who often o'er man's destiny preside;
Unknown to fame, nor borne on rumour's wings,

Yet doing more than conquerors and kings;

They played their part, where pain and want com-
      bined,

And fell despair sat brooding on the mind ;

Where day was night, and night no respite gave,

Earth was no place for rest, and still more drear the
      grave;

Their step was heard, 'twas like an angel's tread.

They wooed the wretched sufferer from the dead;

Night changed to day, the skies again were blue,

Hope on the face of heaven a golden rainbow drew,

And faith on cherub's wings a bird of promise flew.

Nor are these acts alone acknowledged here,

Far in yon vast, where sphere embraces sphere:

There, there, amid the mansions of the skies—

Where seraphs hymn celestial melodies—

Such noble deeds by loftier harps are sung,

Their worth in every heart, their names on every
      tongue.

    Beneath a tree, whose overhanging wood

Pressed the soft bosom of the swelling flood,

Two beings sat in youth's luxurious prime,

Who all unheeding whiled away their time;

And naught in heaven above nor earth below,

The bird's rich song, the wave's melodious flow,

Could for one moment steal upon their sense,

So charmed it was by love's sweet eloquence.

Oh! Spirit, said Adolphus to his guide,

Say, who are they who seek the murmuring tide,

For much from their abstracted mood I deem

That love is all their thought, and love is all their
        dream?

   Adoria answered: On your fruitful earth

Those happy spirits once partook their birth,

Together mingling from their early youth,

Grew mutual confidence and love in both;

But cruel death, which has so often strewn

The opening flowers that gentle love hath sown,

The much-longed union of the pair forbade,

And silenced each beneath the silent grave;

Too strong for death, too strong for time or space,

The kindred spirits now resume their wonted

     place ;

Such are the lofty principles that move

The generous mind, and such the power of love.

    Oh ! teach me, Spirit, if I may presume,

So far beyond the silence of the tomb,

What bond exists between the happy here,

And those who dwell in yonder earthly sphere?

For much I long to know the laws which bind

Corrupted matter to the God-like mind.

    Fond child of earth, Adoria made reply,

To pass the bounds of dread mortality,

Companion of a spirit, and explore

New fields of truth on this sublimer shore,

Is not enough for thy aspiring soul,

But thou would'st learn of hidden truths the

    whole;

So may'st thou gather that celestial fire,

And boundless longings loftier souls inspire ;

But neither thou nor they can ever gain

The immeasurable height at which you aim;

Though gifted with a seraph's daring will,

And fixed resolve and strength invincible;

Far as the eye can reach, and higher yet,

Innumerable worlds in order set,

Are as remote from the great source of all.

That is or was, as yon terrestrial ball;

The soul, with her undying energy,

Resolves besetting doubts, and hails futurity;

But as her vital functions grow more rife,

And burns more fierce the godly life of life,

The theatre enlarges to her gaze,

Fresh, and still brighter worlds, amid the ether blaze;

New hopes surround her in her daring flight,

And thought darts forward with increased delight;

On cleaving wings the thirst of knowledge grows,

The empire for research no limit knows:

But what by greater patience I have gained,

Or from celestial intercourse obtained,

I will, if you so wish, in brief reveal,
Nor from a mortal heavenly truths conceal.

Know, then, the soul is not an aimless thing,
Unseen, unknown, beyond imagining;
Now habiting a frame of southern fire,
Fierce passions and inordinate desire;
Now in the regions where the light of day
But rarely gilds the cold and lifeless clay;
Chained, like a phantom, now to fell disease,
Or dwelling in a form of downy ease;
In all life's torture or ethereal trance,
The wayward child and ruthless sport of chance:
Nor is she driven through tracts of liquid air,
And bound to naked rocks, the victim of despair:
In each dread flight, and in each mortal state,
Ruled by the iron tyranny of fate,—
But, through all being, whether earth or sky,
The founder of her own immortal destiny.

When to chaotic matter form was given,
And chimed the silver stars amid the tower of heaven;

When man from earth, and mind from Godhead
    sprung,
And the new-born creation sweet orisons sung,
Two principles were planted in the breast—
The one of good, and one of ill possest—
And, placed o'er these, like a presiding God,
Impartial conscience fixed her calm abode:
She knows the various spirits who prepare
Intestine troubles and perpetual war;
The sons of light with rays of glory shine,
Their look, their promptings, and their voice divine,
While those of darkness she reveals to sight,
And strips them of their borrowed robes of white;
With these the soul in moral strength may soar
From stage to stage of being, and explore
New mines of virtue, rich in virgin ore,
Or sink degraded in the scale with those
Each vice still pregnant with unnumbered woes.
The body, which the soul her mansion makes,
A portion of her vital power partakes;

Such full emotions through the arteries run,

Such genial heat is borrowed from that sun ;

But when to other spheres the mind ascends,

Her short connection with the body ends ;

A worn and blasted form the mortal lies,

And never more with gifted life to rise :

Yet deem not that the soul thus ends her race;

Though rolling years the tablet may efface,

Those who illustrious live and nobly die,

Obtain a passport to a purer sky ;

Each thought, each action, and each uttered word,

Bears in a future state a just reward :

Hence these, the children of this clime, have been

In other worlds and other landscapes seen ;

Have nursed the twin-born sisters, hope and fear,

And unrequited love and cold despair ;

Some rose superior to the ills of life,

While others sunk beneath the deadly strife.

Oh ! not alone to those who won a crown

Of laurel wreaths, and trophies of renown,

This rich inheritance in prospect lies—

For nature's sons, though weak, may win the prize :

The seeds of truth and virtue, sown below,

Here to a royal tree, and spreading branches grow.

MUTABILITY.

WHEN locked within the surges of the sea,

These sister Islands undiscovered lay,—

When beasts of prey, and reptile shapes abhorred,

Lurked in the woods, nor knew their rightful

     lord,—

Far in the east, beneath the tropic sun,

The warrior reined his steeds, and bards his actions

     sung.

    Snatch, Muse, from out the iron grasp of time,

A few short records of that race sublime,

That, thus disclosed, misguided man may cast
A longing look upon the gorgeous past,
And learn that time sweeps like the mighty sea,
Whilst tempest-drifted, shifting sands are we.

 First sing of Egypt, with her golden soil,
Where threefold harvests crown the peasants' toil;
Where stately Nile her tranquil course pursues,
And steeps her banks with oft-recurring dews;
Or like an eastern conqueror rolls along,
While tributary waters round her throng,
And rich with spoils braves Ethiopia's sand,
To pour them in the lap of her beloved land.

 But well, though nature hath performed her part,
She owns herself surpassed by nobler works of art,
Transmissive relics, which with one accord
Proclaim the strength of earth's primeval lord;
O'er these stupendous towers of ancient sway
A thousand years are as a passing day.
Here sacred pyramids invade the skies,
And shades of Emperors in pomp arise;

Embalmed in state, with spices and perfume,
Immortal is their reign, immortal is their tomb.
Here stand the temples and the dread abodes,
Where dwelt the venerated demi-gods,
Osiris, fountain of diurnal light,
And Isis, empress of the silver night,—
She to her steadfast votaries revealed
The wonders of the heavens, to common mortals
    sealed.

    Lake Mœris hoards the waters of the Nile,
And boasts her famous labyrinthian pile,—
Twelve stately palaces enclosed in one,
Where twelve united kings in regal splendour shone;
Within the dome were built twelve spacious halls,
And countless chambers ranged around the walls;
Each to the other had a secret door
The most observant eye could ne'er explore;
But such as dwelt on the enchanted ground
Could touch each spring, and range the mansion
    round.

In pompous state Diospolis appears,
Towering majestic through the waste of years;
The buried cent'ries 'neath her shadows lie,
And still her massive columns threat the sky.
Here colossean monuments arise,
And living sculpture meets the ravished eyes;
On Luxor's temple, wrought with art divine,
A thousand chariots of the conqueror shine;
The flying steeds and lashing charioteer,
And god-like hero, with his glittering spear;
The trembling Indian flies or shuns the blow,
The javelin gleams on high, and terror reigns
    below.
Nor here alone, but 'mid the dreary waste,
Are seen the stern mementoes of the past:
Imperial cities that in triumph stood,
And plains once fruitful 'neath the teeming flood.
    Behold the great Sesostris from afar
With sound of thunder comes, and trophies of the
    war;

From Danube's banks to Ganges' utmost bounds,

The fame of his victorious arms resounds;

The warlike Scythians and the Thracian bands,

And Asia's legions, countless as the sands,—

Nor walls of triple strength, nor gates of brass,—

Nor mighty rivers, nor the mountain pass,—

Could stay the warrior in his full career,

The walls he stormed, and broke the threatening

      spear.

Innumerable captives round him throng,

And bear the spoils of feudal states along ;

The vanquished kings and princes of renown,

In purple vestments clad, and golden crown,

Are harnessed to his high triumphal car,

And four abreast drag on the conqueror;

When thus upon his lofty seat he rode,

The awe-struck nations shook, and took him for a

      god.

    But turn we hence, nor pause we now to tread

The downward path successive kings have led ;

Enough that wretched serfs and Arab thieves
Defile the temple of immortal Thebes;
And such are the mysterious laws of fate,
A slave sits on the throne where proud Sesostris
  sate.

Hail, mighty Babylon ! in dread we see
The doom of Empires shadowed forth in thee;
Thy grand prophetic voice, in tones sublime,
Comes peeling through the colonnade of time,
And tells vain mortals what mean ends await
All that is beautiful, adored, and great.
How proudly by Euphrates' swelling flood,
With massive walls and lofty towers she stood;
Of all the teeming East the ruling state,
From whom e'en Emperors received their fate,
Their tributary gold and silver brought,
And works of art, and jewels highly wrought.
 The mighty founders of the nation were
Enthroned on monuments in every square,

With those who had immortalized their name
By rightful government and deeds of fame;
The various acts by which their worth was
    known
Inwrought on slabs of rosy marble shone.
Here Nimrod, pride of the Assyrian race,
Through pathless jungles heads the furious chase;
With poisoned arrows pierces those who fly,
And they who wheel around on glittering falchions
    die.
Insatiate, thus he claims unbounded sway—
Men are his hounds and monarchs are his prey.
But Ninus wanders from the track of men,
And seeks the maddened lion in his den;
The noble beast, undaunted, stoops to spring,
The trembling forests with his thunder ring,
The monarch of the woods the king defies,
And holds him with the magic of his eyes,
Till rising, like his rival, with a bound
He pins the roaring monster to the ground.

Semiramis a nobler act performs,

And stands unmoved amid a sea of storms.

Returned victorious o'er her foreign foes,

She skilful workmen and mechanics chose

To build a town, whose battlements should lour

Upon the banded world, and dare its utmost
  power.

Then stately Babylon began to rise,

And charm the artizan's admiring eyes ;

They strain each nerve, in mutual bands combine,

Struck by the grandeur of the vast design ;

But Discord from her ruined cavern flew,

Hissed with her forky tongue, and baleful venom
  threw.

The restless thousands catch the direful pest,

Sedition rears its head and reigns in every breast ;

To overthrow the state their souls conspire,

And set the royal edifice on fire.

The queen had risen from her downy bed,

And from her bath her train of handmaids led,

In conscious pride before the toilet stood,

When clamouring crowds came thirsting for her
blood.

Straight at the news she issued forth alone,

Her eyes with more than wonted lustre shone;

With palpitating bosom glancing bare,

Long trailing robes and wildly flowing hair,

A Goddess thus she seemed and more than Goddess
fair.

Touched at the sight, rebellion melts away;

Where'er she bends her steps the crowds obey,

Abashed before her royal presence fall,

While death-like silence brooded over all.

　　　Fair Amytis, a queen of tender years,

Surveyed the pleasing sights through falling
tears,

In silken fibres wove her life away,

And gazed reluctant on each opening day.

The partial king alarmed, the fair one pressed

To show the cause of sorrow in her breast.

" It ill becomes me," Amytis replied,

" A new-admitted guest, a king's imperial bride,

To shun the splendours of the regal court,

Where gratulating kings and peers resort ;

But know, O King, unheeding and alone,

Though thousands wait around, I mount the
      scarlet throne.

The haunts of youth unsought before me rise,

And Media's landscapes greet my longing eyes,

The sweet meandering footpaths through the
      woods,

And, straying in the midst, the lucid floods.

These halls are bleak, the gilded chambers bare,

While I no longer breathe my native air."

The king, who prized her more than all the train

Of amorous nymphs who sought his love in vain,

Revolved her wishes in his anxious mind,

And then a work of costly care designed.

" Oh ! cease to weep," he cried, and took her hand,

" The vanished glories of thy native land,

As fairy scenes shall Babylon disclose,

And bowers as lovely, curtained by the rose."

Hence the suspended gardens had their rise–

Though propped on earth a smiling paradise.

Arches on arches in procession tower,

Upreared on pedestals of massive power;

On these the circling terraces were spread,

And marble stairs from one another led.

The nearer heaven the lofty flight ascends

The more of glory with the landscape blends.

'Twas here Belshazzar held his impious feast,

Supplied with all the dainties of the east.

The guests by thousands thronged the entrance halls

And ante-rooms that lay around the walls.

The signal given, they crowd through corridors,

And glide with lightsome step along the marble
        floors,

Ascend the steps with gorgeous paintings hung,

While louder and more loud the greeting trumpets
        rung.

In order ranged, they feast on viands rare,

And fruits that only glow in Eden's balmy air.

High in the midst the purple throne was
    reared,

From whence the festival in glittering pomp
    appeared ;

Beneath, the royal table was outspread,

And here the king and peers the sumptuous ban-
    quet led.

A troop of bright-eyed virgins wait around,

Their bosoms decked with flowers, their hair with
    fillets bound.

    The feasting over, mirth usurps the hour,

And skilled musicians try their rival power;

They spread the praises of the god-like king.

With loud acclaims the vaulted arches ring :

High seated on his throne, with golden wand.

The king himself waves his approving hand.

Again, and yet again, the song goes round,

And louder still the vollied shouts resound.

But who are these amid the cypress groves,

Who Orpheus-like lament their absent loves?

I know them by their black eyes anguish riven,

And snowy arms and hands imploring heaven :

The daughters of Jerusalem are they,

Sweet is their voice but mournful is their lay ;

They sing the glories which they see no more,

And court the muses on Euphrates' shore.

For one short space they catch the heavenly fire,

And wake with feathered touch the silver lyre ;

They hail the heights of cedared Lebanon,

And Jordan's waves that through the valleys

　　　run ;

They feel as if inspired, and pant with hope,

Though timid as the milk-white antelope.

But soon aside their much-loved harp is flung,

And their scarce-uttered words hang trembling on

　　　their tongue.

　The drunken monarch rolls his wanton eyes,

And drinks the melody with vast surprise.

Then thus : " if so their harp-strings can entwine,

Haste, bring the vessels that adorned their shrine;"

The courtiers hear the mandate with applause,

Uproarious mirth rides rampant through the halls :

The bowls with sacrilegious wine are crowned,

And thrice are filled and thrice are borne around,

And thrice the muffled thunder shakes the solid
  ground.

The heathen knew the sign, his blood forsook

Its wonted course and ghastly waxed his look,

And like an aspen leaf his frame convulsive
  shook.

A deadly tremour runs throughout the hall,

A god is in the midst, a hand is on the wall.

Scarce had the fatal characters been read,

And scarce the withering doom around been
  spread,

When, louder than the whirlwind's hollow roar,

The Persian and the Mede came rushing through
  the door.

Scarce had the stricken monarch left his throne,
And scarce the hurrying chiefs around him shone,
When stretched a mangled corpse he lay upon the
    stone,—
A worthless thing, as worthless is his fame,
And Babylon is but an empty name.

But say, must proud Euphrates mourn alone,
And Nile and Latium's stream their ancient glories
    gone ;
Are there not other states well known to fame,
As noted in their day, whose cradle was the main ;
Who not on horses and armed men relied,
Or mighty cities walled on every side,
But who upon the wild unbridled vast
Their richest ventures and protection cast ;
Who o'er the dread abyss as fearless ploughed
As darts an eagle through the rolling cloud?
Not least of these Phœnicia proudly boasts
The queen of ocean born upon her coasts.

Her enterprising sons on rafts first rode,

And to their early peril future safety owed.

Along the mercantile levant they cruise,

Now vending purple dies, and now extorting dues;

But when the taper mast light pinions bore,

They flew before the winds and left their native shore,

Passed sacred Cyprus and the Cretean Isle,

And hailed the Herculean famous pile.

Like roving pirates here and there they land,

Despoil the natives, toss the flaming brand;

At times persumptuous seize a royal prize,

And bear a princess off before her father's eyes.

But soon these acts of lawless outrage cease,

And the surrounding nations live in peace;

They hail the pennant which they feared before,

And with their native produce crowd the shore.

The skilful navigators trace each sound

And tract unknown, and ride the depth profound;

Inspect the isles of the Œgean sea,

Ionian coasts, and fruitful Sicily.

The islanders, with wondering awe, admire
The flying vessels stored with rich attire ;
The various produce and designs unfold,
And for the tempting tinsel yield the sterling gold.

  Encouraged, thus along the neighbouring seas
Sprung teeming marts and thriving colonies.
Arabia sends the produce of her lands
By Median traders o'er the burning sands,
Her frankincense, and myrrh, and spices rare
From toiling caravans perfume the desert air;
The merchants watch the purple heavens from
   far,
Their heightened glory and their guiding star ;
The pangs of thirst and hunger are controlled,
For nature's thirst is quenched in greater thirst for
   gold.
From Egypt pulses, and from Palestine
Choice garnered wheat and soul-inspiring wine,
And silken wool from flocks as white as snow,
And oil, balm, honey, which those realms bestow.

There Indian Ophir sends her gold and gems,
To grace like stars the imperial diadems ;
And pearls and ivory from a far-off shore,
Where rival currents meet and mighty oceans roar.
Armenia, coursers of unrivalled breed,
Trained to the chariot, and of lightning speed ;
Hespania, silver from exhaustless mines,
And corn, and luscious fruits, and choicest wines ;
From Cyprus, timber for the lashing oar,
And tin, where Cornish waves in sounding breakers
        pour.
    High on her rocky throne secure from fate,
Her satellites around, the peerless mother sate,
Surveyed the produce of the fruitful earth,
Proud of her sea-born race, and in her conscious
        worth;
In one hand grasps the treasures of the east,
The other hoards the bounties of the west ;
The suppliant nations view the matchless queen,
Her sweeping garments and majestic mien ;

With tasteful art she spreads her wares around,

Her regal gifts by mutual gifts are crowned;

Each state with pride the novel store surveys,

And the deluded world unbounded tribute pays.

    Such was her power, when from heaven's
        sapphire throne

Her future was decreed, her final ruin shown.

The Almighty ruler shook his vengeful rod,

And earth and hell confessed a more than heathen
        God.

As when the stately moon with borrowed light

Glides through the spacious firmament at night,

And spreads her silver glories o'er the sky,

All worship and admire her silent majesty ;

But when her full-blown beauty fades away,

And slender grows her form and dim her vestal ray,

Unnumbered spheres along the heavens are seen,

And pallid and forlorn moves on the crescent queen :

So with proud Tyrus, when her God withdrew

His countenance, whence all her greatness grew,

Each wasting war, and more disastrous peace,
Beheld her glory wane, her boasted wealth decrease:
Till, whelmed beneath the fatal stroke of years,
A ruin here and there is all that now appears.
Her sole fond lover, the Levantine wave,
Still hovers near and howls above her grave,
With mourning weeds bedecks his hoary head,
And lays her relics in old ocean's bed.

But not unsung fair Carthage shalt thou be,
Thou great by land, thou empress of the sea ;
'Twas not enough that with an eagle's sway
Thou mad'st the peoples of the coast obey.
Ambition led thy armies to explore
The realms that lay far distant from the shore ;
To plant thy banners on the Alpine height,
And force the Latian foe on Latian plains to
      fight :
Then, when the nations, with dilated eye,
Bent forward to behold the crowning victory—

To mark which race was of celestial birth,

And which should wield the trident of the earth—

Thou did'st forsake thy son mid doubtful wars,

And tear his laurels by domestic jars ;

He moved to grasp an universal crown,

Thou, not the Roman, struck his right arm
    down :

An exile in barbaric lands he roamed,

But still with noble pride his country's fate be-
    moaned—

That fate which, gathering on the horizon's brow

Black with destruction, threatens even now ;

When, after bearing wrongs in every form,

Thou half provok'st yet fear'st the rising storm.

    The cruel Romans goad their prostrate foe,

Intent upon her final overthrow,

And, on a slight pretence, their legions pour

Like swarming locusts on the Punic shore.

In vain the Carthaginians look around

For men and arms, alas ! no friends are found.

"Ah, where the magic of this golden wand,"

She cries, " that marshalled armies on our strand ;

Then sprung spontaneous at my early call

Numidian horsemen, and the bands of Gaul,

Balearic slingers who, removed afar,

Ply whizzing stones that rattle through the war,

The Spanish troop, and stedfast Genoese,

And Grecian heroes, born beyond the seas :

Not one responds of all my warm allies,

Dumb is the earth, and deaf the partial skies."

    Then shook her seers, then fell her haughty

      eye—

She hears the Latian taunts, nor makes reply.

Hushed is the battle shout, the vaunted boast,

She bends, she kneels, and silent is her coast ;

Her fighting men rely on war no more,

They lay their weapons down, and clemency implore.

Unmoved, the foe beholds the sight forlorn,

Accepts the proffered arms, and then replies with

      scorn.

Too late she finds that they who would be free
Must hold themselves erect and dare mortality.
No act so mean but she would undergo
To shield her fair possessions from the foe ;
But now the treachery that she had taught
Falls on her head with tenfold vigour fraught ;
The Romans claim her city and her lands,
And doom her sons to dwell mid desert sands.
She hears, but scarce the words can comprehend,
Till, felt at length, her lamentations rend
The brooding clouds, and to the heavens ascend ;
But friend nor foe now heeds her piercing cries,
Nor interpose the sullen deities :
When, rising frantic from her abject prayer,
She feels a courage lighted by despair,
Her sons more lofty tread, and with emboldened
     air.
    And now the clangour of the trumpet warns
The coming strife, and each his fellow warms,
Tumultuous shouts are heard, and ring of forging arms.

The city, quenched beneath the Roman ire.

Glows a vast furnace of embodied fire,

And withering blasts from iron lungs respire.

Roused, like the ocean by the whistling blast,

The citizens to tower and rampire haste,

Spears, javelins, missiles, thicken in the sky,

And every soul is steeled to win or die ;

The matrons hurry, with dishevelled hair,

To draw the bow, and common danger share ;

And maidens, in luxuriant mansions bred,

Twine into ropes the ringlets of their head.

Meanwhile, the horsemen issuing on the plain.

In squadrons charge, and wheel, and charge
     again.

The more the stern besiegers press the foe,

The more resources the beleaguered show.

Oh, could the conqueror of the Alps awake,

And once again the Roman legions shake ;

Assume the power, the thunders of a God.

As when sublime on Tiber's banks he trod ;

Then would the fates reverse the cruel doom,
And Tyrian fires light up imperial Rome.
But vain the wish to animate the dust,
Or scour the mail of penetrating rust ;
And vain, when heaven and earth in wrath combine
To save the remnant of a failing line.

    And now within the walls gaunt famine rears
Her ghastly head, and with her train appears ;
Confusion, tumult, terror, and despair,
And pestilence and fever harbour there,
And shrieks of maniacs pierce the startled air.
At length the tottering battlements succumb,
The bold defenders drop down one by one ;
In rush the exulting foe with blazing brand,
Shines the reflecting sea, and glares the rocky strand.
Red flames fly crackling o'er the crowded street,
And gathering, mount in one unbroken sheet,
Till heaven and earth in dire combustion meet.
The wretched citizens distracted run,
Nor know which fate to seek, or which to shun.

Some, unappalled, spring headlong in the fire

To appease dread Saturn's unrelenting ire;

Some plunge to Triton's vulnerable abode,

And sink beneath the waves they once in triumph

    rode;

These unresisting meet the victor's spear,

While those on their own arms conclude a mad

    career;

The rest, a miserable degenerate throng,

Are driven, like bleating flocks, the public streets

    along.

In sordid rags, half-famished, they appear,

And old decrepit men bring up the flagging rear.

And shall imperial cities in a day

Fall from their height, nor leave a parting ray;

Shall states that reared an universal throne

Be chronicled on history's page alone;

Shall races to succeeding races yield,

And they in turn be forced to quit the field;

And man not gather from the shifting scene
What rocks to shun, what whirlpools intervene ;
What gentle currents to the rapids lead,
What treacherous sands the pilot's course impede ?
Are signals set along the stormy main
To warn the sea-tost mariner in vain ;
Does he, in spite of these, the breakers dare,
Lured by its light, or dazzled by its glare ?
And shall the statesman, with averted eye,
Turn from the paths which lead to victory,
And seek the realms of darkness and decay,
With ghosts his guides, and wrecks of empires in
      his way?

A nation, like the vulture, is at first
On naked clifts mid cloud and tempest nurst,
With danger for her dower.   The hardy race
Pursue the toil and triumph of the chase ;
Their frames are cast in nature's sternest mould.
With iron limbs, and muscle fold on fold.

At length they sip the vintage of the plain,

Though nauseous to the taste they sip again—

A charming poison sparkles in the bowl—

They drink huge draughts and drown the free-
born soul.

" Ah, why," they cry, " exist on barren rocks.

When corn and wine are near, and tempting
flocks."

Swift the contagion spreads, the shrill alarms

Along the mountains ring, and call to arms—

Not fiercer whirlwinds bluster in their cave,

Or foaming cataracts their channels lave.

They sweep before them in their furious course

The foeman's enervated foot and horse ;

The fields are cleared, the peopled cities won.

And now the second epoch has begun.

Moved by necessity, the common voice

Proclaim a king or rulers of their choice ;

The new-formed government new costumes wear.

As kings usurp, or crowds the sceptre share.

F

But when domestic cares and turmoils cease,
And the smooth wheels of justice glide in peace,
They hear the envoys who arrive from far
With friendly greetings, or for help in war.
This cause and that with pride they undertake,
And on the issue their own fortunes stake.
Reared on the rocks invigorating height,
And armed by science for the coming strife,
They march to victory where'er they tread—
Their prowess and renown o'er all the earth is
　　　spread.
New tracts are joined to their extended sway,
The proud they humble, and the great obey.
A race of Cæsars in full triumph come,
And pile their spoils within another Rome.
A boding calm sits on each gazing state,
As nature were o'ercharged by so sublime a
　　　fate.
　　But now she pauses in her bright career,
She stays her chariot, and she rests her spear,

No fond ally demands her vengeful arms,

No threatening state her own repose alarms,

But from her midst a more insidious foe

Assumes the reins and works her overthrow.

The road is paved with luxury and sloth,

Rust eats her sword: her purple, silken moth.

Vice and corruption on her features brood,

And avarice dries the fountains of her blood;

Yet still her car moves on 'mid glittering sheen,

And golden trappings on the steeds are seen,

And jewels on her sunken breast appear,

And bays upon a forehead carved by care.

They who behold her with unheeding eye,

Deem her the prototype of royalty;

And still she rules the nations by her fame.

The prestige of her arms, the terror of her name ;

But those who watch her, mark her as the prey

Of sure destruction and of foul decay.

Awhile she lingers, as the gaudy light

Flares for a moment, sinks, and all is night.

Triumphant Albion ! on thy past renown
Lay not thy queenly robe and starry crown;
One fell reverse away that prop may tear,
And leave thy head exposed, thy snowy bosom bare;
Nor count thy fair possessions in thy need,
For they will yield thee but a broken reed, —
The teeming Indies which thy rule obey,
Where Dynasties have ruled and passed away;
Nor Australasia, pregnant with her gold ;
Nor Northern tracts, which arctic waves enfold;
Nor fortresses, nor rising colonies;
Nor islands dotted o'er the swelling seas,—
Will spread their arms to save you as you drown,
But spurn thee or conspire to drag thee down.
Nor on thy wealth and commerce place thy hope,
For when thy fleets with rivals cease to cope—
These having bred an artificial thirst,
And useless hands and populations nurst—
Will turn to famine, turmoil, and despair,
The sure precursors of internal war.

Nor will alone thy trading weave for thee,
With foreign states, the bonds of amity;
Though int'rest is the gordian knot of friends,
Imperial treaties serve imperial ends ;
An Alexandrian sword will force the hold,
For naught can melt ambition into gold.

But in the greatness of thy soul confide—
Thy inborn strength, thy sons of martial pride—
On virtue's dower, of more transcendent worth
Than all the treasures hoarded in the earth;
But chiefly on thy God, who, throned on high,
Controls the spheres and spans the boundless sky,
Beneath whom kings and empires are as dust :
To Him exalt thine eye, in Him repose thy trust.

SPRING.

Hail, gentle nymph! I know thee by thy deep
  Blue eyes of tenderness, and golden hair;
  By all the primroses that cluster there;
By the sweet blossoms that begin to peep
From out their fastnesses of winter sleep.
  By thy all-conscious cheek, and bosom bare,
  Wooing the dalliance of the wanton air,
And the deep sighs thou should'st in silence keep.
I know thee by thy ever-varying charms,—
  Thy syren voice amid the myrtle grove,
  Soaring to eloquence in songs of love,
  Till the stars answer from their orbs above.
And last, I know thee by the fond alarms
With which thou fall'st into thy lover's arms.

SUMMER.

RECLINING on a bank of blushing roses,
  Fanned by the zephyr's undulating wing,
The lady summer in full bloom reposes,
  All eloquent with love's imagining.
Soft silvery sleep her drowsy eyelids closes,
  And round her the sweet birds in rapture sing,
Whilst her deep heaving breast too well discloses
  The burning thoughts which to her vision cling.
But, hark ! loud rumbling on his dusty car,
Her lord approaches from the fields of war.
  A moment, and his muffled thunders roar,
And his winged javelin glitters from afar;
  A moment, and those martial feats are o'er,
  Dropped are his arms, and all is peace once more.

AUTUMN.

A MOTHER sat within a lowly cot,
   With mossy rose and honeysuckle bound;
   Smiles played upon her features, as the sound
Of prattling feet were heard—a happy lot
Was hers; past trials and sufferings were forgot,
   For her sweet children gathered all around,
   And warm embrace and hearty welcome found.
The earth contained no care, the sky no blot ;
But lo ! a tear now starts into her eye,
And deeply heaves the oft-recurring sigh ;
   For those dear children fade her eyes before,
And a deep solemn warning passes by,
   Like dungeon chains upon some desert shore;
   And knock, knock, knock, and Death is at the
     door.

WINTER.

A poor old man am I, bereft, forlorn;
   My children and my spouse are gathered home,
   And I am left to totter on alone,
Without a hand to guide, or breast to warm.
The spring and hey-day from my life are shorn;
   My voice hath ta'en the dreary dungeon tone,
   And like a worn-out pilgrim on I roam,
With haggard look, and garments rent and torn.
And yet at times faith opens to my eye,
   And a voice whispers comfort through the gloom;
The snow-drop and the daisy glisten by,
   Like bright thoughts round the precincts of the
      tomb;
And often 'mid the darkness I descry
Steps of a ladder leading to the sky.

THE STATESMAN.

To rule a nation's glorious destiny,
   To be her star, and chosen oracle;
   To draw her friends, her enemies repel,
Uphold a righteous cause where'er it be;
To keep his country, or to make it free,
   And without firing passions none can quell;
   Arouse the people, with a mighty spell,
To guard their own, and rule by land and sea,—
This is a proud ambition, and when gained
By honest means, and by such means maintained,
   Will make him great who to such height can
      tower.
But woe is he who, when he hath attained
   His cherished wish, forsakes at such an hour
   The love of country for the love of power.

HOPE.

THOU art a mighty genius, who can'st fire
  The hearts of all men with thy silver ray;
  A star to light the pilgrim on his way,
And make his lowly thoughts to heaven aspire ;
A martial goddess, who midst ruin dire
  Dost lead thy victims to the dubious fray,
  And promise them the laurels of the day,
But when the fight begins thou dost retire.
I, too, have been thy votary, but to me
  Thou didst play false and loose, and never more
Thy deep blue eye and beckoning hand shall be
  The bright inveiglers which they were before,
For on the margin of life's troubled sea
  I trace thy wrecks and broken faith of yore.

MUTABILITY.

TRACE through thy changeful life, and thou shalt see
    Engraven on each passage, and each deed,
    On all thy purposes, which were the seed,
The darkened scroll of inconsistency.
    Recal the friends who left thee in thy need ;
    The love that beckoned, while it made thee bleed,
And read the spectral word—inconstancy.
    Think o'er the thoughts which crowded wave on
        wave,
    Then broke amid the echoes of the cave,
And sank beneath the sands of memory.
    But lo ! thy pulse now trembles, can'st thou brave
    The tyrant, who would lead thee as his slave,
    With fettered hands and chains, unto the grave,
And carve upon thy stone—mortality ?

TIME.

Now soaring on the eagle's wings sublime,
　Like the destroying angel thou dost sweep ;
Now prowling wolf-like at the midnight chime.
　When all the world but thee is wrapt in sleep,—
　Thou dost an everlasting banquet keep,
And spendthrift of thy fortune, stealest mine :—
　For ever sowing where thou can'st not reap,
These are thy attributes, destructive time.
　But say, O heartless squanderer ! why so bold ?
　Is not thy fall and very death foretold ?
A conqueror, thou soon shalt conquered be ;
　E'en now methinks that thou art waxing old,
And when thou diest who will mourn for thee,
Thou craven slave to proud eternity ?

IMMORTALITY.

AWAY, presumptuous man ! thy sophistry
　　Awakes no echo in my conscious soul ;
　　For it hath springs and depths beyond control,
Which ne'er were fathomed or explored by thee.
Tossed on life's wild unfathomable sea,
　　Where tempests threaten and the wild waves roll,
　　We need a needle pointing to the pole—
So points the soul to immortality.
Thou ask'st for proof—know, there are truths
　　　　sublime,
Felt by all races, known throughout all time,
　　Which need no proof—like bright stars as they
　　　　shine,
They stand confessed ; then raise thee in thy prime,
From stage to stage in moral grandeur climb,
　　Nor deem a brute, what God hath made divine.

THE SAXONS' BANQUET.

The banquet was set, and the cymbals prepared ;
And the Saxon and Briton right heartily fared.
The King, and the nobles of England were there.
And Hengist, and Horsa,—Rowena, the fair.
  And friendship and mirth are reigning supreme,
  O'er the minds of the revellers, met on the green.

Rowena, the pride of the King, sat in state,
And round her the fairest from Germany wait ;
The King of the Britons stood bound like a slave,
By the girdle of love, by the glances she gave.
  And Venus, the goddess, is reigning supreme,
  O'er the minds of the revellers, met on the green.

The bowl passes onwards,—away and away
Fly the dreams of the past, fly the cares of the day;—
They rise and they fall, and they shout in their glee,
As free as the winds, or the waves of the sea.
　And Bacchus, the god, is reigning supreme,
　O'er the minds of the revellers, met on the green.

The Saxons now stand in a cluster apart;
There is scorn on their lip, there is blood in their heart;
Again and again their proud glances they cast,
Like vultures or wolves, o'er the flagging repast.
　And treachery reigns like a demon supreme,
　O'er the minds of the Saxons, now met on the green.

The King of the Britons arose from his throne;
Bade the music proceed, and the revel go on:
They rise and they fall, and they sing and they shout,
But hark! there are footsteps and voices without.
　And dread, and confusion, are reigning supreme,
　O'er the minds of the Britons, now met on the
　　green.

The clashing of spears, the surprise, the alarm :—
The shouts of the monarch, "Arm, arm, Britons
    arm !"
The groans of the dying, who fall as they fight,
Gave a terrible close to the banquet that night.
  And horror and carnage are reigning supreme,
  O'er the Britons and Saxons, now met on the
    green.

The timid young morn, like a bride of the sea,
Peeps over the ocean, and smiles on the lee.
" 'Tis morning, 'tis morning," the merry waves ring,
" 'Tis beautiful morning," the little birds sing.
  But death, like a phantom, is reigning supreme,
  O'er the nobles of Britain, who met on the green.

DEATH OF HAROLD.

THE morn hath pierced the curtains of night,
And chased the stars with his darts of light,
To gaze on a field where all shines bright,
　　In battle's proud array.
Spears, helmets, and crests, are glittering there,
And banners unfurled, and stout arms bare ;
And shouts of defiance ring thro' the air,
　　And court the dubious fray.

They come ! the proud Norman knights of old,
In steel-clad armour, and crests of gold,—
Like waves of the ocean, stern and bold ;
　　An empire for their stake.

Then arm thee, Harold! and take the field,

Set the revel by, and thy battle-axe wield,

And bind to thy arm thy ponderous shield;

    Awake, awake, awake!

Hark! even now the trumpet hath rung,

And threatening knights on their chargers sprung.

Singing the songs that Roland sung—

    The bard of Charlemagne.

Then rouse thee, Harold! in all thy power,

And bring to the front thy country's flower;

For blows, thick and fast as a thunder shower,

    Shall join the battle's clang.

Mid shouts of the Briton, and shouts of the foe,

And clash of the battle-axe, blow for blow,

And banners high waving o'er corpses below,

    The dreadful day sweeps on.

Till night, like a bird of prey swoops down,

With ruffled plume, and with deadly frown:

Where now is the King, and where his crown?

  Hark to the minstrel's song:—

" No more to meet in the banquet hall,

The bravest and best among them all;

With the turf his grave, and the sky his pall,—

  Lone, lone, O doubly lone!

Stretched where the drooping willow weeps,

And his sons and nobles lie in heaps;

With his crown still grasped, King Harold sleeps.

  Gone, gone, for ever gone."

SONG OF RICHARD CŒUR DE LION

IN CAPTIVITY.

Away, away, I will not heed
  That melancholy strain ;
The notes of triumph will succeed
  While pride and hope remain.
The mighty spirits of the past
  Around their mantle fling ;
And breaking through these chains at last,
  I yet shall be a King.

Time was, I sat upon a throne,
  The sceptre in my hand,
And shall I ne'er reclaim my own ?
  Again a monarch stand ?

Yes, though a wretched captive now,
    A poor degraded thing,
With wreaths of laurel round my brow,
    I yet shall be a King.

Princes and knights have followed me,
    In those proud days of yore ;
And shall I lead to victory
    And feats of arms no more ?
Yes ; for I hear the battle-shout,
    The axe and broad sword ring,
The Saracen in utter rout ;—
    I yet shall be a King.

Then scorn for scorn I throw thee back,
    Thou recreant in the fight ;
A Duke of Austria ! well, alack !
    But ne'er a Christian knight.

Oh ! that I had thee face to face,
   Within the listed ring,
Thou soon would'st end thy coward race ;—
   I yet shall be a King.

But thou, a brother of my blood,
   To find thee what I've found !
E'en vultures watch their savage brood,
   By laws of nature bound.
But thou hast seized upon my crown—
   Yet doth not conscience sting ?
Aye, God will pluck the spoiler down ;—
   I yet shall be a King.

The waters sweep the castle walls
   With a melodious lay ;
And morning, like a spirit falls
   Upon the cold damp clay.

And perched upon the lattice high

I hear the wild birds sing

Of faith, and hope, and liberty ;—

I yet shall be a King.

THE INTERVIEW
BETWEEN BRUCE & WALLACE
AFTER THE BATTLE OF FALKIRK.

'Twas eve, and o'er the western hill
  The sun shot forth a parting glance;
And all around grew dark and still,
  As folded in a death-like trance,
When on the banks of Carron's flood,
Two gallant knights in armour stood.

" Hail ! gallant knight," the younger cried ;
  " None more renowned than thou in war,
None bolder through the battle ride—
  Of all the chiefs the guiding star.
Endowed with stern, unbending will,
Which baffled oft, is soaring still.

" Yet pause thou in thy reckless course,
    The desperate die is cast in vain;
What is thy poor distracted force
    To match a mighty monarch's train?
Thou add'st but fuel to the fire,
And wak'st still more the victor's ire.

" But if ambition fire thy breast,
    And bid thee do all man may dare;
A crown will never yield thee rest,
    For thou a nation's curse shalt bear.
Thy slaughtered friends in troops will rise,
And call for vengeance from the skies."

" Hold!" shouted Wallace, "hold thy own,
    I battle not for selfish ends,
Nor envy kings upon their throne;
    Methinks 'tis thou should'st make amends,
For thou hast leagued thyself with those
Who are thy country's ruthless foes.

" Lo ! strewed upon yon gory plains,
    Lie Scotia's nobles, side by side ;
They scorned to wear a tyrant's chains,
    But like the Roman nobly died.
Doth not their dust e'en now rehearse
On traitors' heads a nation's curse ?

" Rise, Bruce, redeem thy ancient name,
    Thy country will her wrongs forget ;
And children's children shall proclaim
    Thy glory when thy sun hath set.
Rise, Bruce, and for the past atone,
Hearts, arms, await thee, and a throne.

" But if thou still would'st be a slave,
    And pride thee in thy foul disgrace,
Go, sink unnoted to the grave,
    Save as a traitor to thy race.
For me, I scorn to join the throng
Who triumph in our country's wrong.

" The woods, the mountains of the land,
    The rocky islands off the shore,
Are open all at my command,
    Where I may hold my own once more.
There will I sit and mourn for thee,
And dream, at least, my country free."

He said no more, but strode away,
    Fast followed by his gallant band ;
Bruce gazed upon their proud array,
    And seemed irresolute to stand.
Such stern reproach he ill could brook.
And his whole frame convulsive shook.